10 Minute Tales

THOMAS & FRIENDS

Based on *The Railway Series* by the Rev. W. Awdry

When you see these symbols:

Read aloud
Read aloud to your child.

Read alone
Support your child as they read alone.

Read along
Read along with your child.

EGMONT
We bring stories to life

Read aloud   Read along

It was a beautiful day on the Island of Sodor, and Thomas the Tank Engine was chuffing cheerfully along to Tidmouth Sheds.

On his way, some children stopped to wave to him. "Hello, Thomas!" they called.

"Hello, children!" he peeped happily back at them.

Read alone

Thomas was puffing to Tidmouth. He said hello to some children along the way.

Read aloud   Read along

When Thomas arrived at Tidmouth, he saw Edward and Gordon. They were listening to The Fat Controller.

"This afternoon, there will be a special story time for the children at the library," The Fat Controller said. "I need an engine to collect the brand new books from Maithwaite Station and take them to the library."

Thomas hoped he would be chosen for the job. Listening to stories with the children was his favourite thing to do!

Read alone

The Fat Controller had an important job.
He needed an engine to take some new books
to the library for a special story time.

Read aloud   Read along

"Thomas, you will deliver the books," said The Fat Controller. "Make sure the books are at the library on time."

Thomas was very excited! "Yes, Sir!" he beamed as he pumped his pistons and set off for Maithwaite.

Thomas rushed along the tracks. "I mustn't be late for story time," he told himself.

The Fat Controller asked Thomas to deliver the books. Thomas went to Maithwaite Station to collect them.

Read aloud Read along

Thomas steamed into Maithwaite Station.

"Hello, Thomas," waved the Station Master as he arrived. "You look very happy today."

"I am," Thomas tooted. "I'm collecting the books for the special story time at the library!"

The Station Master blew his whistle. Two large trucks full of books of all shapes and sizes began to roll towards Thomas. The little blue engine couldn't believe his eyes – he'd never seen so many books before!

Read alone

Thomas arrived at the station. There were
two trucks full of books for him to collect!

Read aloud   **Read along**

"**I** must hurry!" Thomas told the Station Master as he was buffered up to the trucks. "I have to deliver these books on time!"

As soon as the trucks were attached, Thomas pumped his pistons and puffed quickly out of the station.

"Wait, Thomas!" the Station Master called after him. But Thomas had been in such a hurry that he hadn't waited for the books to be properly covered. They were loose in the trucks!

Read alone

Thomas raced away from the station.
He didn't wait for the books to be covered.

Read aloud   Read along

Thomas steamed quickly along the track. He whizzed around corners. He whooshed along the straights. He wheeshed across the bridges. He was determined not to be late for the special story time!

But back in the trucks, the books were beginning to jiggle and jostle, and the faster Thomas went, the more they began to bump around.

Read alone

As Thomas went faster, the books bumped around in the trucks.

Read aloud   Read along

As he approached a junction, Thomas could see that the signal was red. But he didn't want to stop! Then an idea flew into his funnel.

"I can take the branch line," he thought. "There aren't any junctions along there!"

So Thomas puffed quickly down the branch line. He kept getting faster and faster, but the faster he went, the more the books jostled and jiggled in the trucks.

Thomas took the branch line so he didn't have to stop. He went faster, and the books bumped around even more.

Read aloud   Read along

When Thomas raced around a bend, he saw a sign warning all engines to slow down because of track works ahead. Thomas was annoyed – he hadn't heard about any works on the track before he left!

"Bother!" he said. "Going slower will make me late!"

But just as Thomas began to put on his brakes, he had a thought.

"If I didn't know about them, then the works can't be big," he thought. "So I will just go through them."

And with that, Thomas went even faster!

Read alone

There was a sign warning engines to slow down. But Thomas ignored it.

Read aloud   **Read along**

Then there was trouble!

As he steamed along at full speed, the uneven tracks made Thomas start to bump and jump. Behind him, Thomas' trucks were bumping and jumping just as much as he was, and the books jiggled and jostled like never before. Some even began to bounce into the air!

"Cinders and ashes!" Thomas cried as he started to apply his brakes.

Read alone

The track was very bumpy. Thomas and his trucks bumped and jumped all along it.

Read aloud   Read along

But it was too late.

Thomas hit the biggest bump of all, and with a loud SNAP the trucks came loose! They flew through the air, scattering all the new books across Farmer McColl's field.

Read alone

Thomas' trucks snapped loose! The books were scattered all over the field.

Read aloud   Read along

Thomas' brakes screeched to a halt and he looked back at what he had done.

"Oh my!" he gasped. "The books are all over the field! Now the children won't have their special story time, and it's all my fault."

Thomas was very sad. He knew that if he hadn't been in such a hurry, he would have arrived at the library safe and sound.

"What am I going to do?" he asked himself.

Read alone

Thomas looked at the books in the field.
There would be no story time now.

Read aloud   Read along

As he looked at the books in the sunshine, Thomas wished the children could see them. An idea bubbled up in his boiler.

"I know," said Thomas. "If I can't take the books to the children, then I'll bring the children to the books for a special picnic story time instead."

Very gently, Thomas puffed away to collect Annie and Clarabel from the Steamworks. He had learnt his lesson about going too fast!

Read alone

Thomas decided to take the children to the books. He went to pick up Annie and Clarabel.

Read aloud   Read along

At the Steamworks, Thomas told Victor and Kevin about his plan. They thought it was a great idea!

Thomas waited to be coupled up to Annie and Clarabel, then he tooted off to collect the children.

At the platform nearest the library, Thomas found all the children waiting for him.

"Jump aboard!" he told them. "I'm taking you to an extra-special picnic story time in the sunshine."

The children cheered as they climbed aboard. They'd never had a picnic story time before!

Read alone

Thomas collected his carriages.
Then he went to pick up the children.

Read aloud **Read along**

Thomas puffed towards Farmer McColl's field. This time, when he reached a red signal, he waited patiently. And he didn't take the branch line with the bumpy track.

When they arrived, the children ran towards all the colourful books in the field. They each chose one to read. They were very happy to be out in the sunshine for their story time!

Read alone

Thomas puffed slowly to the field.
The children were very excited.

Read aloud **Read along**

But Thomas was happiest of all.

He'd managed to give the children their special story time. And as he sat and listened to all the stories, he realised that some things were worth waiting for.

Thomas was pleased. He'd saved story time and made the children very happy!

Read alone